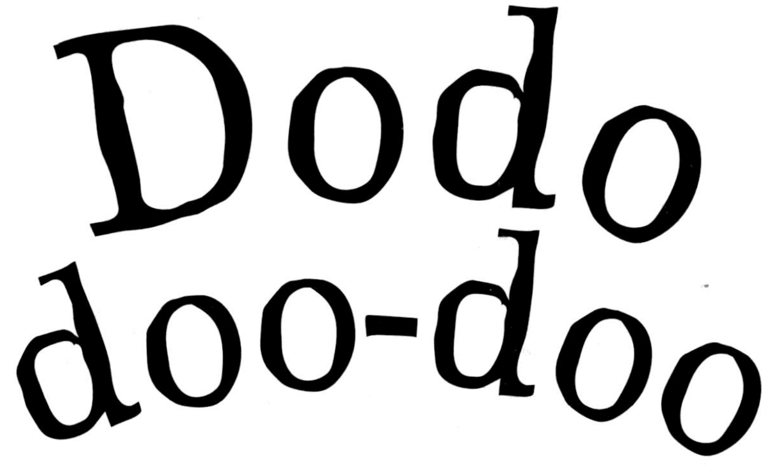

This Dodo Book belongs to:

. . . .

To Mo and Ella ~ K.U.
For Teddy ~ K.P.

First published in hardback in 2010
Published in paperback in 2011
by Hodder Children's Books

Hodder Children's Books,
338 Euston Road, London, NW1 3BH

Hodder Children's Books Australia,
Level 17/207 Kent Street,
Sydney, NSW 2000

A catalogue record of this book is
available from the British Library.

ISBN 978 0 340 95057 9 (HB)
ISBN 978 0 340 95058 6 (PB)

10 9 8 7 6 5 4 3 2 1
Printed in China

Hodder Children's Books is a division of
Hachette Children's Books, an Hachette UK Company

www.hachette.co.uk

ENDPAPERS BY JOSIE MCPHERSON, AGED 10
Thank you to Phil and Jim, Art Club, Oxford
for helping with the endpapers

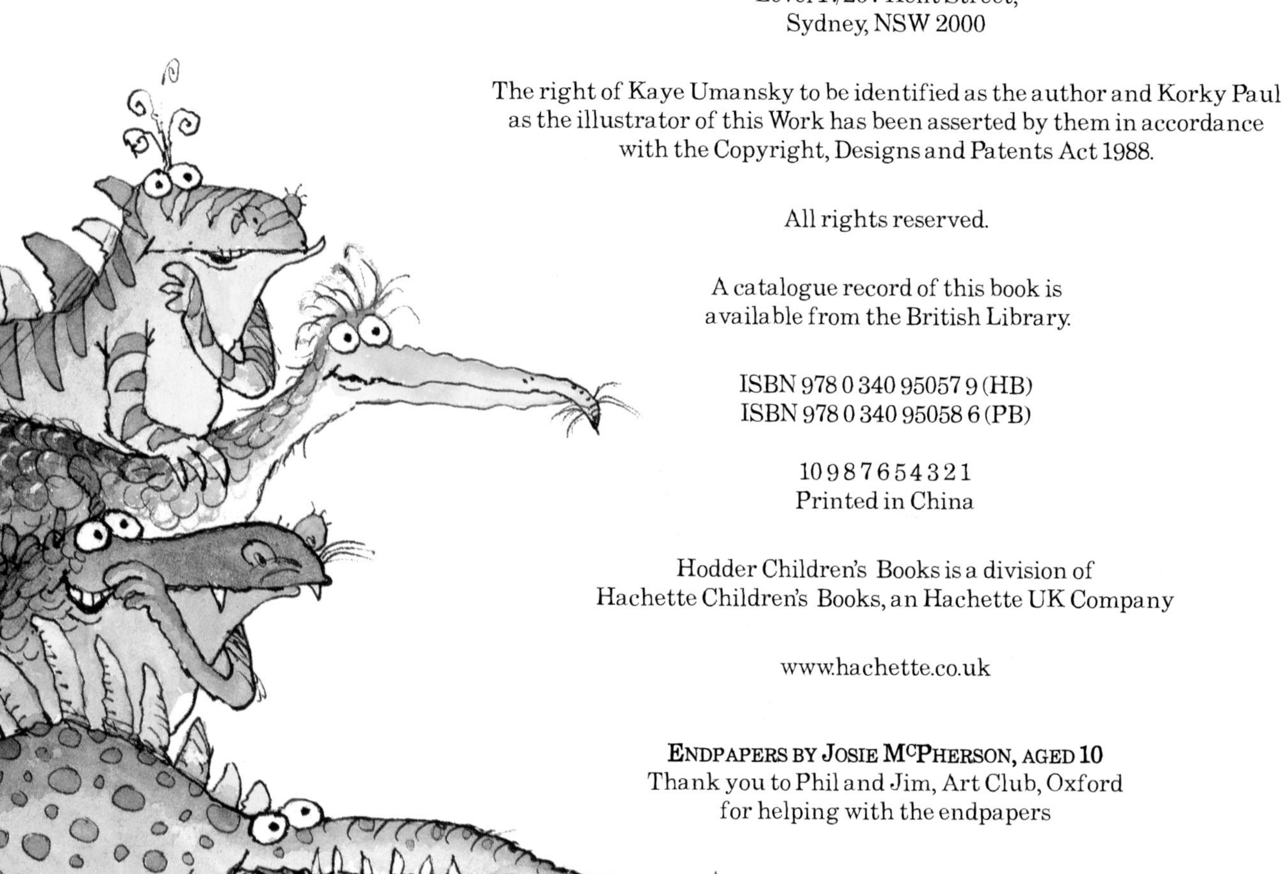

www.kayeumansky.com

Dodo doo-doo

Kaye Umansky and Korky Paul

Hodder Children's Books

A division of Hachette Children's Books

When walking in the woods one day
I met a friend called Fred.
He was going on a Dodo hunt.
Well, that is what he said.

He was carrying a bucket
And a shovel and a rope…
A net, a sack, a bag of chips,
A home-made telescope…

And strapped across his shoulder
Was a most peculiar pipe
That he claimed would make a Dodo noise.
The kid was talking tripe.

'A Dodo hunt?' I said to Fred,
And gave a little sneer.
'There *are* no Dodos in this wood.
You'll find no Dodos here.

For Dodos are extinct, you see.
I know that same as you do.'
'If Dodos are extinct,' said Fred,
'Then what's that Dodo doo-doo?'

He pointed to a steaming pile
That lay beside the trail.
Then he took his trusty shovel
And he plopped it in his pail.

'How do you know that's Dodo doo?'
I asked in some surprise.
He was staring in the bucket
Like he'd won some fancy prize.

'It could be from a chicken
Or a partridge or a quail,
Or any other bird that does
Its doo-doo on the trail.'

'It *isn't*, though. It's Dodo doo,
I know it is,' said Fred.
'And the Dodo that did do the doo
Is somewhere up ahead.'

'Stand back! I'll blow the Dodo pipe
To flush it out, you know.'
He raised it to his eager lips
And gave a mighty blow.

PAAA

A head came first. A head with eyes.
A head with eyes and beak!
Those eyes were wide with shocked surprise.
'Don't move,' said Fred. 'Don't speak…'

'She's BIG!' I said. 'She's **BIG** *and FIERCE!*
I think she just might bite.
I don't think we should hang around.
I think she wants a fight.'

'Oh no,' said Fred, 'the Dodo
Is a gentle sort of bird.
She only wants to hug us.
I'm the expert. Take my word.'

AAA

She CHARGED us from the bushes!
Fred went shinning up a tree.
The Dodo hurtled onwards –
She was heading straight for me!

I dodged around the Dodo,
And I raced towards the thicket!
I hoped to hide somewhere inside.
I hoped that I could trick it.

I didn't see the Dodo doo
Until it was too late.
I found a bit that Fred had missed.
What happened next was fate.

I landed in the nest, you see –
The nest that had the egg in.
I really put my foot in it.
In fact – I PUT MY LEG IN!

I'd smashed the world's last Dodo egg.
That's what I'd gone and done.
The Dodo mum was not amused.
She'd only laid the one.

She pecked my nose, she pecked my knees,
She pecked my scarlet ears.
She wandered off – I don't know where –
Her eyes were full of tears.

Friend Fred came climbing down the tree,
And made a great to-do.
'So Dodos are extinct?' he snapped.
'They *will* be, thanks to you!'

A tragic little story
Guaranteed to spoil your day.
It started out with doo-doo
And went downhill all the way.

I leave you with the moral,
Which is very short and sweet.
If you're out walking in the woods...

…watch where you
put your feet!

Other great Hodder picture books perfect to share with children:

978 0 340 95984 8 (PB)

978 0 340 95985 5 (HB)

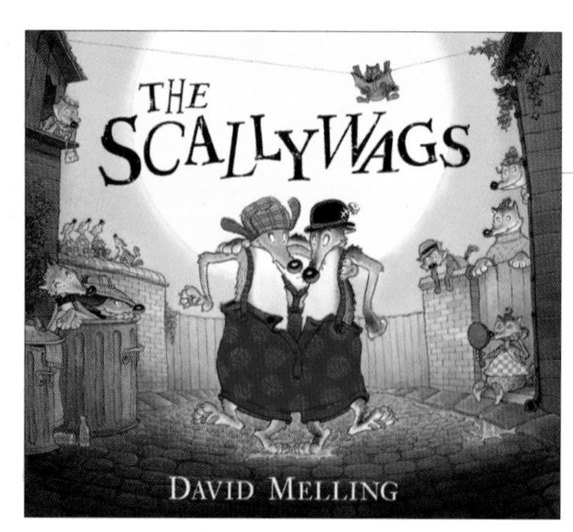

978 0 340 88406 5 (PB)

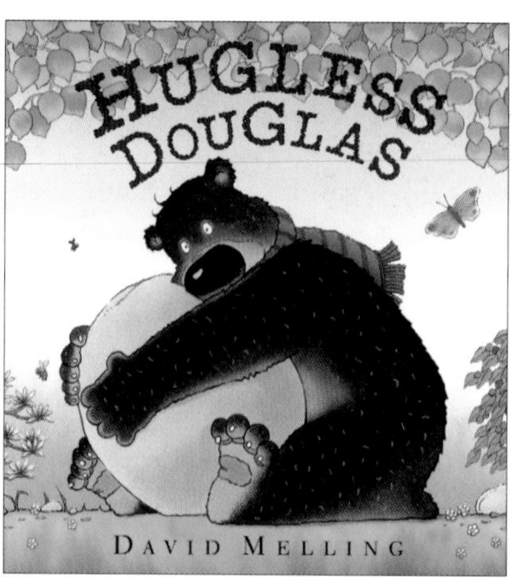

978 0 340 95063 0 (PB)

978 0 340 89329 6 (PB)

978 0 340 98164 1 (PB)